Book 2

Alain M. Bergeron
Illustrated by Sampar

Translated by Sophie B. Watson

ORCA BOOK PUBLISHERS

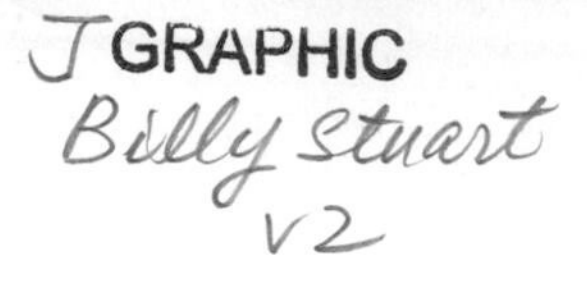

Cataloguing in Publication information available from Library and Archives Canada

Issued in print and electronic formats.
ISBN 978-1-4598-1840-8 (softcover).—ISBN 978-1-4598-1841-5 (pdf).—
ISBN 978-1-4598-1842-2 (epub)

Simultaneously published in Canada and the United States in 2019
Library of Congress Control Number: 2018954152

Summary: In this illustrated novel for middle-grade readers,
Billy Stuart and his loyal Scout group have inadvertently traveled through time
and are trapped in a labyrinth with King Minos's Minotaur.

Orca Book Publishers gratefully acknowledges the support for its publishing
programs provided by the following agencies: the Government of Canada,
the Canada Council for the Arts and the Province of British Columbia through
the BC Arts Council and the Book Publishing Tax Credit.

We acknowledge the financial support of the Government of Canada through the National
Translation Program for Book Publishing, an initiative of the *Roadmap for Canada's Official
Languages 2013-2018: Education, Immigration, Communities*, for our translation activities.

Cover and interior illustrations by Sampar
Translated by Sophie B. Watson

ORCA BOOK PUBLISHERS
orcabook.com

Printed and bound in China.

22 21 20 19 • 4 3 2 1

Table of Contents

BILLY STUART
FOXY
YETI
THE ZINTREPIDS
SHIFTY
MUSKY
FROUFROU

DEAR READER,

Billy Stuart wasn't exactly elected to this particular position. He doesn't wear a magical ring on his finger like Frodo. He doesn't have a secret collection of masks or stones hidden in his drawers like Zelda. He hasn't walked through life accompanied by a daemon like Lyra. Nor does he have a distinctive lightning-shaped scar on his forehead like Harry. Basically, the future of the world does not rest on his thin and bony shoulders.

Billy Stuart is just a young, ordinary raccoon who has experienced some extraordinary adventures.

Here is the second adventure he told me about.

Alain M. Bergeron

One twelfth of January, in the town of Cavendish.

Author's note

First of all, let me introduce myself. I am Alain M. Bergeron, the author to whom Billy Stuart has told his many adventures.

Over the course of these pages, you will notice I feel the need to add my two cents directly into Billy's story, so as to:

- clarify a point or some bit of information;
- add a personal commentary;
- amuse myself;
- all of the above.

My presence in this book and the following ones will be through the use of an author's note. These little interruptions look like a note glued to a page.

And now, you can get back to your reading.

A.M.B

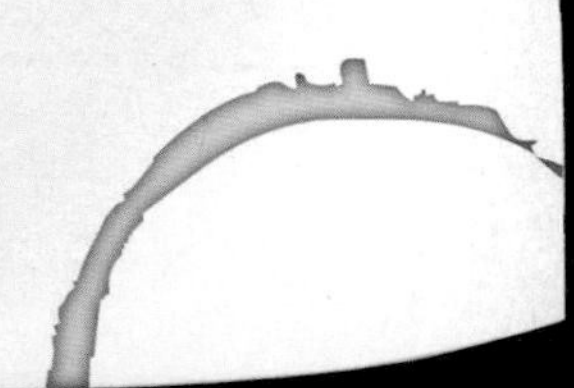

THE RECAP

Billy Stuart has promised to take care of FrouFrou, the MacTerrings' dog, for the whole summer and is dreading the long days of July and August. Then he gets a letter from his grandfather, Virgil, who claims to have found a cave with a passage that lets him travel in time. Billy Stuart sets out on his grandfather's trail, accompanied by his scout pack, the Zintrepids—and FrouFrou. What Billy doesn't know is that once they go down the fateful path his grandfather took, there will be no turning back.

In the course of their adventures, this is how Billy Stuart and his friends, and even the dog, become stranded in another world...in another time...

In the Land of Dinosaurs?

Sitting on a giant **ROCK** at the exit of Belcher's Cavern, I remember the instructions my grandfather Virgil wrote in his notebook:

Get yourself to the heart of the city's maze. You will find there the clue for the next part of your journey.

To figure out WHERE we are, and WHEN, we must first get out of this place. After consulting the Zintrepids pack members, we opt to head north. Judging by the position of the SUN in the sky, it should be around two o'clock.

I lead the way, with Foxy at my heels. She's holding FrouFrou on her leash. Behind her are Musky, then Shifty and finally Yeti, watching our backs.

While we are walking on a trail through the unfamiliar, dense forest, we wonder:

The path descends a gentle slope, and the forest brightens.

"Maybe we are in ANCIENT TIMES? Or the MIDDLE AGES? Or the FUTURE?" Foxy says.

I hear a familiar sound as we approach a bend in the trail—a river!

We cross a meadow of tall grass to reach it. The stream is as wide as a road. And there are no unusual smells. I taste a drop with the tip of my tongue. No bitter taste. It might be safe to drink.

"The water is good!" Shifty says, slurping as he chews up a dragonfly caught in midflight.

Greedily we gulp down the delicious, clean water and fill up our canteens.

Wherever you find rivers and freshwater, you find… crawfish!

Yummy! Yummy! I'm not just thirsty. I am also famished. And those granola bars in my bag won't be enough to fill me up.

A couple of meters from the bank, the water is up to my knees. I can see the bottom of the river. I only need to move a few stones to find my favorite dish. I search and search fervently—I had one! I HAD TWO!

"KABILLIONS of crusty-clawed crawfish in that Bulstrode River!"

A river of crawfish. It is heaven on earth! Is this a part of the Bulstrode River I didn't know about?

"YUM! Such a treat! So delicious!"

I notice a tree trunk heading toward me—which is curious. Normally a trunk would be following the current. This tree trunk is moving in more of a diagonal kind of way.

Whatever! That trunk can do what it wants—my mind is focused on my stomach.

I spot a crawfish trying to escape. I pick it like an autumn apple. It is gigantic. It must be the queen of the crawfish! My mouth waters.

The tree trunk...gets closer. Just then Foxy screeches from the riverbank.

"**BE CAREFUL!** It's a crocodile!"

FrouFrou barks and growls. Musky grabs Yeti by the collar to stop him from throwing himself in the water.

"Bring it on! No, really, bring ***it*** on!

Terrified, I flee the gaping jaws of the CROCODILE… and lose the queen crawfish. *My booty! I'll never find another crawfish that big!* Not an important observation, I know. But I told you already: my mind was on my stomach. I am mourning my lost crawfish when I should be focusing on getting away from that CARNIVOROUS REPTILE.

Enough about the crawfish! I escape the animal's attack at the last second and scream:

"Troop! Quick! Throw him the dog! It'll distract him!"

"**Really, Billy Stuart, really??!!!**" says Foxy, who knows more than anyone how much I don't like FrouFrou.

There are more human deaths attributed to hippopotamuses than to crocodiles. However, I couldn't find any statistics about crocodile aggression toward raccoons.

By the way, I am way more agile than a **tree trunk**, even one powered by a massive tail! I leap onto the crocodile's back and from there throw myself out of the water to a safe spot on the bank.

"All that for a miserable crawfish," Foxy **SCOLDS**.

"My guilty pleasure, I confess," I say, still panting.

FrouFrou starts **BARKING** and **GROWLING** again. The crocodile is now on firm ground and moving quickly in our direction. He seems pretty determined not to lose such an appetizing dinner.

An adult crocodile can live up to two years without feeding itself. Apparently, this one was hungry...

"***RUN!***" Musky shrieks.

We are practically tripping over our own feet as we clear out of there.

We've barely gotten away from our assailant and passed through a meadow of high grass when we come face-to-face with **ARMED SOLDIERS**.

TOPSY-TURVY

Sometimes our friends the Zintrepids worry about where their next food will come from, but they usually go from **FEAR** to a **MEAL** in only a few words.

In the game Metagram (meta=transformation and gram=letter), you get from one word to another by changing one letter at a time, each time creating a new word. For example, you can get from **SORE** to **HORN** like this:

SORE-BORE-BORN-HORN

Turn the word **FEAR** into the word **MEAL** by creating new words between them.

HERE ARE THE RULES:

 You can only change one letter per word.

 The letters must stay in the same order.

 The words can be singular or plural.

 Each step must involve a proper word.

Write down your words on a piece of paper so you will be able to see the solution more clearly!

Solution on page 158.

Ancient Times

The presence of soldiers confirms one thing: we are not in the Age of Dinosaurs.

> It's only in the realm of fiction that dinosaurs and humans rub shoulders. Several millions of years separate the disappearance of one and the appearance of the other.

"**OUCH!**" Musky says as he touches the **tip** of a soldier's spear. "It's the real deal!"

A dozen soldiers surround us.

Yeti challenges them. "Bring it on! No, really, bring *it* on!"

"Spray them, Musky! Spray them!" Foxy begs while trying to ***STOP*** FrouFrou's pulling.

The poodle is all excited, wagging his tail and hopping up and down on his hind legs. He wants to meet the strangers.

Musky, the one we accuse every time we detect a bad smell, declares:

"Oh, so *now* you don't want me to hold it in?!" She says it with her snout in the air.

Based on the uniforms, helmets and sandals of the soldiers, I presume we are in ancient times. Or on a **MOVIE** set depicting ancient times, in which case the wardrobe stylist would deserve an award for the accuracy of the costumes.

But I am convinced no one is going to yell, "**CUT!**" Which is lucky, because I don't want to get chopped up! You know, with all those spears...

We are now prisoners of a patrol of soldiers who must have been born a few dusty millenniums ago. We could be in the era of Julius Caesar. Oh! With luck we might even meet the queen, Cleopatra!

Follow us!
Where are you taking us?
To the port! Move along, skirt-wearing raccoon!
It's not a skirt, it's a kilt!
Commander Troudos!
There's a crocodile on the riverbank not far from here.
Go kill it for me! We will make some shoes for the governor and a purse for his wife!
That will put them in a good mood.

To finish up with crocodiles, it's been reported that in the last sixty years, nearly 20 million have been killed. Today they are protected—talk about a story of saving their skin!

The soldier quickly leaves. He returns ten minutes later to present himself to his commander, looking a little banged up.

"Um...the crocodile didn't want to cooperate, my captain. He refused to be turned into sandals."

"**Imbecile!**" His superior spits, then barks, "Keep moving!"

Quick-footed soldiers surround our group. We don't dare slow down, because all slowpokes get their behinds pinched to keep them moving.

We emerge from the forest. A large cart pulled by two robust horses is stopped near a dirt road. Uninvited, FrouFrou jumps on board and settles himself COMFORTABLY on a cloth that's covering wooden crates.

The convoy moves forward. We march like this for an hour. Sometimes the poodle lifts his head and **BARKS** and **WAGS** his tail when he spots us. The rest of the time he rests his paws on the edge of the cart, tongue hanging out, and enjoys having his head in the wind.

He has four legs! That dirty, dolled-up mutt could walk like the rest of us!
Stop your moaning! He's only little, my dear, lovely FrouFrou!
Hold me back, Billy Stuart, or I will fight all of them. Bring it on! No, really, bring it on!

?
!?!
?
Yes, that's it!
Hold me back, otherwise...
Commander, he's staring at me!
Me too, Commander! There's something shady about this guy.

Commander Troudos sighs and curses. What did he ever do to deserve such a group of hopeless nincompoops?

Meanwhile I am busy trying get information from my neighbor, the one who confronted the CROCODILE.

"Tell me, sir, what year are we in?"

He looks at me like I've said something really **stupid**.

"What year? What do you mean?"

"Are we 500 years before Jesus Christ? Or 200 years after Jesus Christ?"

The soldier doesn't miss a beat. "What's this 'Jesus Christ'?"

Our discussion has taken a turn I didn't expect. I explain.

"He had a major impact on the history of the world. We redid the calendar to the year zero when he was born. There was a *Before Him* and an *After Him*."

"I've never heard of him. **DON'T FALL BEHIND**, or I will get punished by my commander."

"And why are we headed to the port?"

The soldier **SMILES** menacingly.

"We have a delivery for the island of Crete."

ANAGRAMS

By changing the order of the letters in a word, you can create a new one. For example: react = trace, warms = swarm

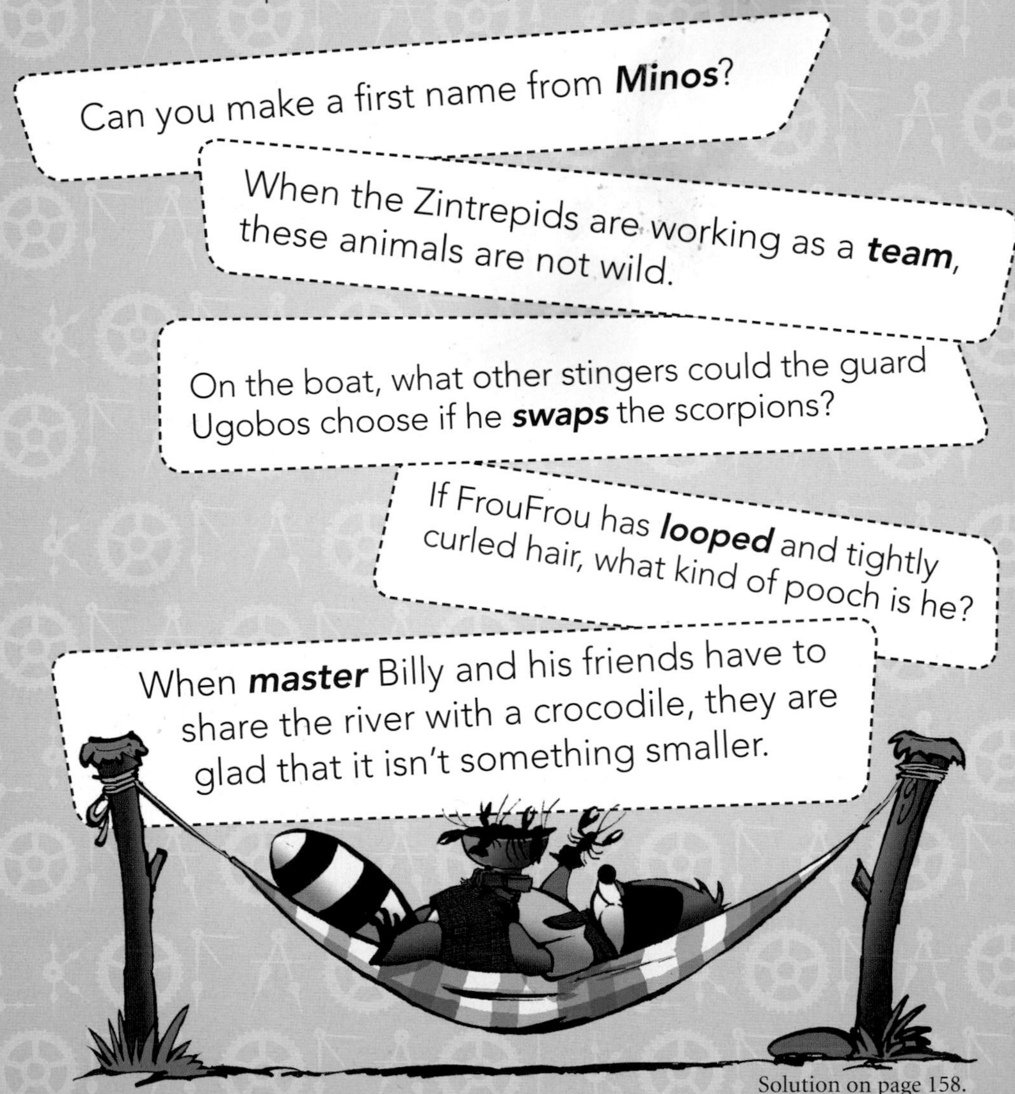

Solution on page 158.

An Unhappy Ship

After barely escaping the murderous jaws of a crocodile, we had fallen into a patrol of soldiers. They march us to a port near a city.

Sadly, I don't think this is the city my grandfather mentioned in the message in his notebook: *the heart of the city's maze…*

Because, there is no actual city, only a few fishing cabins. Come to think of it, it isn't really a proper port either. It's more a makeshift camp for sailors on holiday. A third-class pit stop. The gangway that brings us on board the ship is rickety and UNSTABLE. We can't walk it more than two at a time. Loslobos, the captain of the ship, greets us COLDLY.

"What is this?" he asks the commander of the patrol, Troudos, who is ahead of us.

"A present for Minos for your **VOYAGE** to Crete. I'm sure he will appreciate it—especially the dog!"

The captain looks us over from head to toe with his dark black eyes.

"A raccoon in a skirt?"

I correct him. "Sir, it's a kilt."

"Hmmm," he says, stroking his beard like it helps him think.

Troudos hands him a sack containing pieces of gold.

"A little something for the disturbance, captain..."

Satisfied, Troudos leaves the ship to join his men on the ground.

Large **black sails** are deployed for the castoff. But the wind fails us after an hour, and we have to row. They assign us places in the vessel's galley among some other young people, barely older than teenagers and all clothed in *long red robes*.

I share the bench with a rower who acknowledges me with a brief nod. A **whip** snaps beside me, motivating me to start rowing.

"Get to work, you band of no-good, do-nothing lazy loafers!" bellows the guard, Ugobos. A short-legged, potbellied guy dripping in sweat, he is just waiting to give us a taste of his medicine.

Behind me, Shifty sings to himself:

Row, row, row your boat...

Row, row, row your boat...

Yeti starts to sing. He isn't even able to sit on his bench—he's simply clutching the oar as it swings around. He's been paired with a very large rowing partner.

Musky and I join in, and soon we are all singing. The song seems to give us strength and help our rhythm. We start rowing faster. Ugobos is just about to use his **whip** to quiet us down when the captain stops him.

"Don't—the SHIP is going faster. Leave these poor things alone."

Reluctantly Ugobos tucks the whip away.

"You're too good to the prisoners, Captain," the guard accuses.

Loslobos gives his underling an **icy stare**. "Never question my orders!"

When the guard resumes his position, I strike up a conversation with my neighbor.

"Why don't we have leg irons on?" I ask.

“They’re unnecessary. The captain has banned them. Can you imagine what would happen in a shipwreck? No one would be able to escape from the boat.

“But even if you did escape, the sea is massive and infested with SHARKS and other strange creatures.”

My fellow rower is named Zeppelinos, and he is Athenian. He tells me he's part of a group of young people who were chosen to be sent to Crete to be **sacrificed**.

"Sacrificed!" I yell, terrified. "**KABILLIONS** of crusty-clawed crawfish in that Bulstrode River!"

This ***ADVENTURE*** reminds me of something else. I need to try to sneak a word in with Foxy. She loves history, and I need to learn more about this era.

Little Beasts

Not surprisingly, the rowers resume their naturally slower rhythm once the singing stops. Ugobos finds another way to motivate us to pick up the pace: little beasts!

The rowers cry out as the guards let loose…A BUNCH OF SCORPIONS!

"Don't you dare let me see you stop rowing!" Ugobos says menacingly. "The captain is sleeping at the moment. If he hears one single moan, he will wake up, and that would definitely **ruin** my good mood."

"Try not to move," Zeppelinos advises me.

I pass the message along to my friends. It is only Yeti who isn't able to sit still on the bench. Hooked onto the oar, he scans the boat and looks the tiny creatures in their eyes.

"Bring it on! No, really, bring *it* on."

I can sense the other rowers getting **NERVOUS**, and then they all fall quiet. I dread hearing the first moan of pain from one of us.

SCORPIONS are similar to crawfish, aren't they? Why should I be scared?

Because there is one on the bench, very, very, close to me!

"Move slowly toward me," **WHISPERS** Zeppelinos.

The scorpion, pincers open, stinging tail ready to make fire, seems to be looking for just one sudden movement from me to justify his attack.

Slowly, very slowly, I distance myself from the beast, all the while continuing to row. Zeppelinos snuggles up against the galley wall to give me extra room. The scorpion ignores my attempt to give it space and advances toward me anyway. I know Ugobos is watching what is happening. He **sniggers** with pleasure. If I am stung, the pain will make me scream. I am a reasonable raccoon, but the pain

will definitely force me to stop rowing. Then I will be whipped. I'm worried this is about to get seriously unpleasant.

I am so scared!

I squeeze my eyes shut to stop the **tears**.

Wh...what?

Where is the scorpion? Gone? What happened?

I hear the **AWFUL** sound of a body being crushed. I look at Shifty, who has just finished chewing the little beast…

> I was going to write *biting with his teeth*, but that would have been incorrect because chameleons don't have teeth. Which doesn't stop certain ones from stuffing themselves with scorpions in the special way that meerkats do. (Did you know that meerkats eat scorpions?!) Remember, dear reader, Shifty is a chameleon unlike any other.

The scorpion's tail is hanging out of my friend's mouth. He grabs it and tosses it under the bench.

I had no idea Shifty was so hungry. He catches and swallows a dozen more scorpions that were scurrying around this part of the ship.

The Revelation

The captain, Loslobos, gives his orders for docking at the port of Knossos. In just a few MINUTES we will hit land. A sad expression passes over his face as he looks at the people he has to deliver at the port. Zeppelinos whispers to me, "He must be thinking of his sister, Timoree."

A few months ago, he tells me, another group of Athenians was taken to the island. Loslobos's sister was part of the group. Strange tales circulated around the country about a MONSTER and human sacrifices.

This story is sounding more and more familiar.
Young victims...
A monstrous creature...

I'm getting déjà vu...

Where is Foxy when I need her? There! Busy cuddling FrouFrou. What a **waste** of time!

I join them and summarize the situation for her. As soon as he spots me, the dog **bounces** around, barking. I take advantage of an apple core left on a barrel and chuck it over the side of the boat, to get some peace.

SPLASH!

"Go get it!"

Foxy glares at me. I bat the air like I'm swatting a pesky fly.

"He could always dog-paddle to the shore," I say.

I tell her about my conversation with Zeppelinos.

FrouFrou's leash—where did it go?
Um....we...ah! Forget about it! It was lost at sea, okay?!

Give to Caesar what Caesar is due, and to Foxy what is Foxy's. In our class at school she was awarded the title "Student We Should All Try to Be Like."

The fox searches her memory. She has to think about what is unique about our current situation and then remember a story she read in **our time** that is taking place TODAY.

A glimmer in her eye tells me she is on the right track.

"Crete...young people...a monster...it's..."

Her eyes widen in **HORROR** like they did the time she saw me without a kilt. I'm not sure I want to hear her answer.

"The **monster**," she stammers. "It's the..."

A clamor arises on the wharf where the boat has stopped. A crowd has come to welcome the victims.

"The what?" I say to Foxy, screaming to be heard above the noise.

A gangplank is brought to the ship so we can disembark. Armed **SOLDIERS** cool their heels on the wharf. They are there to escort us. A hush falls as the king, Minos, arrives.

The monster is the MINOTAUR!

King Minos

Foxy's cry paralyzes the crowd and TERRIFIES the soon-to-be sacrificial lambs, including me.

"KABILLIONS of crusty-clawed crawfish in that Bulstrode River!"

This group of young Athenians has been delivered to appease the hunger and temper of the MINOTAUR!

I thought the half-human, half-bull monster imprisoned in a labyrinth only existed in the HISTORY BOOKS. I shake just thinking about it.

As the astonishment passes, Yeti starts boxing an invisible enemy.

"Bring it on, Miniature! No, really, bring *it* on!

No one thought to correct the weasel. Of course, it was the Minotaur, not the miniature. Perhaps Yeti thought the Miniature was the Minotaur's kid and that he'd finally get to fight someone his own size.

We are herded to King Minos who is seated upon a portable platform. We are expected to throw ourselves at his feet. The king looks at us with curiosity.

"What's that?" he asks.

"It's a **kilt**, sir. Not a **skirt**."

The king mocks my answer.

"No, what I meant was, are you the first course or the dessert?"

He bursts out laughing. One of his advisers explains to him that we were captured by a **PATROL** outside Athens.

These foreigners are a present from Commander Troudos!
Foreigners! Our traditions demand that you must first enjoy our hospitality.
Why does the MINOTAUR eat Athenians?
Why aren't there any people from Crete on his plate?
Probably because the monster doesn't like the taste of cretins! The Minotaur loves more exotic cuisine!
We are Cretans, not cretins! You cretin!
CLAC!
Destination: Town.

Foxy, how does the Minotaur story end?
As I remember, it was Theseus who volunteered to go defeat the monster.
Theseus? She's going to save us?
It's a him, not a her.
Is one of you Theseus?
No.
No.
What's this business about Theseus? BE QUIET!

I whisper to Foxy, "Theseus. He kills the Minotaur?"

The fox lowers her eyes and gives an embarrassed laugh. "I don't know. I stopped reading—I was too scared."

We've been walking for thirty minutes when FrouFrou joins us. He is **inexhaustible**. Excitedly he hops up and down, unaware of the fate that awaits us. He leaps up and snuggles into Foxy's arms.

Zeppelinos edges his way over to me.

"Once you are inside the labyrinth, you need to stay in a group," he advises. "People say it's incredibly easy to get lost in the maze. It's so extensive it's like a city."

As soon as Zeppelinos says the words **maze** and **city**, I have a flashback to my grandfather Virgil's note: *Get yourself to the heart of the city's maze. You will find there the clue for the next part of your journey.*

Yes!

To get out of here, we will have to find the clue at the center of the labyrinth and avoid the Minotaur. It's our only hope.

The Labyrinth

As we approach the labyrinth, which is near King Minos's palace, the crowd starts chanting:

"Yum! Yum! Yum! Yum!"

I assume this noisy demonstration has one goal: to let the Minotaur know his dinner has arrived. He must already be licking his lips.

From the hill high above the labyrinth, we have a good view of the maze's impenetrable structure. It is mind boggling—it looks like a city made of stone.

To the eye, it is at least ten times BIGGER than our sports field at school. How will we ever find our way? We'll be playing cat and mouse with the Minotaur inside. The monster must know every nook and cranny of the maze!

"Maybe we'll be lucky and he's hibernating," said Musky. "Maybe it's winter here—"

A **HORRIBLE** cry comes from the labyrinth, alarming us.

GROOOOOOOOOOOOAAAARRRR!

"I'm afraid that spring has come," I say, "and the beast has woken up."

We march down the hill and stop in front of the DEADLY trap. A crowd has filled the amphitheater to watch the dismal spectacle.

An opening in the stone wall leads into the labyrinth. The corridor inside the entrance is obscured by darkness.

From his lofty platform, the king snaps his fingers. A silhouette emerges from the labyrinth. We hold our breath.

The **MINOTAUR**? No, just a man clothed in rags. He welcomes us with warmth and compassion. He introduces himself. "I am Ronos, guardian of the labyrinth."

He gives us **TORCHES** and lights them to help us see our way. "The walls have been built to deliberately stop the light of day from illuminating the maze," he explains.

Minos lets out a contemptuous laugh.

"My poor Ronos. What does it matter if they can see? No one has ever come out of the labyrinth. Right, folks?"

"*NO ONE!*" the crowd cheers.

"We have a motto that I think is brilliant," Minos adds. "*When you go in, you never go out!* You'll be amazed! Ha! Ha! Ha!"

Ronos shakes his head miserably.

Poor Ronos. I promised him my daughter's hand and my fortune if, miraculously, someone actually manages to make it out of the labyrinth.
Crowd, are you watching?
YESSSSSS!
Enough talking! Guards, bring our guests to the banquet...
...the Minotaur's banquet!
You! I want the dog!
He's the same color as the walls in my daughter's bedroom.
Hey, me too! I can be the same color as the walls of your daughter's room!

KAiiii!
!!!

FrouFrou!

Not now...

Good luck and goodbye!

From now on, there is no turning back.

THE ENIGMA OF THE CROSSING

The Zintrepids are in distress. They are stuck on the south bank of the Bulstrode River, and they absolutely have to get to the north bank, but the rowboat they are using can only hold 12 kg (26 lbs). On top of that, at this time of year the water is infested with carnivorous piranhas (at other times of the year, they are herbivores).

"I have an idea," says Billy Stuart. "We could just throw the dog in the water! It would create a diversion, allowing us to swim across!"

"Really, Billy Stuart!" reprimands Foxy.

How can our friends succeed in crossing the river?

Clues:

MUSKY AND SHIFTY ARE THE FIRST TO BOARD THE BOAT. THE REST IS UP TO YOU TO FIGURE OUT…

But what about FrouFrou? You must be worried!

"He'll swim!" says Billy Stuart. "Don't worry! You know that Foxy will rescue her darling little FrouFrou. Which is too bad for the piranhas." Billy Stuart sulks. "I'm sure they are hungry…"

A Compass

We venture deep into the **BELLY** of the labyrinth. I walk in front, clutching my torch. Foxy, distracted by FrouFrou's disappearance, holds her torch over her head and peers into the darkness. The passages are high enough and WIDE enough that we can walk in scout formation, side by side in pairs.

I hear barks coming from far, far behind us. Goodbye, calf, cow, pig, chickens and FrouFrou!

Billy Stuart just recited part of a line from Jean de La Fontaine's fable *The Milkmaid and the Pot of Milk.*

If one day we emerge from this nightmare, it will be weird to go to the MacTerrings and tell them their dog was adopted by the daughter of a king in Crete over 3,000 years ago.

Strangely, the barks are getting closer.

"FrouFrou!" calls Foxy.

New thought—it will be weird to go to the MacTerrings and tell them that a Minotaur ate their dog. Does a Minotaur cook its food before eating it? Does it like cold dogs or hot dogs?

Excited by the reunion with Foxy, FrouFrou, who has actually outfoxed the guard, pees on the ground. He sniffs it and barks happily.

"FrouFrou is marking his territory," Foxy says while giving FrouFrou extra cuddles.

I can't help my sarcasm. "I'm sure the Minotaur will be terrified!"

"Don't be scared," says Shifty, rolling his eyes around. "I am looking both backward and forward!"

"Yeah," adds Yeti. "The Minotaur? Pfffft. I could eat one every day for breakfast. Bring it on! No, really, bring *it* on!"

The passage slopes to the RIGHT. Four new passages are in front of us. Which do we choose?

A GROWL makes our blood run cold.

"It's coming from there," says Musky, pointing to the opening on the far left.

"No, from this one," says Foxy, in front of the next opening.

"You are all wrong. The scream is coming from the third opening," Shifty says. "You can trust my sense."

From where I am standing, in front of the opening on the right, I'm sure the noise is coming from somewhere over here.

"We could each choose a passage," Yeti suggests. "That way our chances of finding the EXIT will be better. Unless you're scared of being alone?"

Objections arise.

"No way, Yeti! We could lose each other. We need to stay together."

In scary movies, characters get picked off one by one because they split up. I don't want that to happen to us!

"Which passage shall we choose then?" asks Musky.

"I'm sure they all lead to the Minotaur, so let's try to get to the heart of the maze to find the clue before the monster finds us."

"WAIT!" Foxy warns.

She rummages in her bag and takes out...a COMPASS! Using this instrument, we will improve our chances of not getting lost. Foxy consults it in the light of her torch, looking for magnetic north. She is quickly disappointed.

"It's demagnetized! The needle is moving around like the second hand on a clock," she complains.

"It's probably due to the magnetic personality of the host of these here parts," Shifty says.

FrouFrou starts feverishly sniffing the ground around the four openings. He hesitates, sniffs, turns around, sniffs again, searching for something….

Suddenly Foxy announces, "Look! Our compass!"

I tease. "That's it! Foxy, you've lost the **POINT**."

"What do you mean?" Shifty asks.

Foxy points to the dog. "Haven't you read the classics? In ***ASTERIX AND CLEOPATRA***, it's the dog, Dogmatix, who helps the main characters, Asterix, Obelix and Getafix, get out of the pyramid."

Foxy is referring to the world-famous Asterix series, created in 1959, written by René Goscinny and illustrated by Albert Uderzo. There are thirty-plus titles in the series, and *Asterix and Cleopatra* is the sixth adventure of the famous Gauls. They were the subject of a cartoon and a film by Alain Chabat, which was very funny. And René Goscinny is my favorite author.

"Listen, *we* don't have a magic potion like they did in the story."

"But, Billy Stuart, we have FrouFrou! The poodle can act as our four-legged compass. His sense of smell will help us find the exit. He just has to pee to mark our path."

On hearing his name, FrouFrou bounds around me. I rub his head.

"Go! My bea—" I choke on the word *beautiful*. "Go, doggy, go pee!"

FrouFrou continues to jump, excited for the attention I'm giving him.

"Dog! Do a nice pee-pee. You are capable, my bea"—no, it's too hard—"my dog. Psssssssssssss."

I lift my paw and pretend to pee to encourage him to imitate me.

"You're gross, Billy Stuart!" Musky says, laughing.

I sense my patience starting to wane.

"Imagine, dog, that you are at our house. And there are visitors…you know the puddles you like to leave on the floor…"

I might as well be talking to a **STONE GARGOYLE**!

"Silly mutt!" I clearly have no problem saying *that*. "You could make yourself useful for once! Do you need a **fire hydrant?**"

FrouFrou barks and spins like a **top,** chasing his short tail.

"No! No treats! Just a pee-pee!"

Foxy intervenes. She caresses the head of this annoying dog.

"My beautiful FrouFrou, go pee, please."

Right away, he sniffs the GROUND in front of the four openings and stops in front of the second one from the left. He lifts his leg, and everyone claps. Except me. I grumble.

"He was missing the **MAGIC WORD**," Foxy says, laughing. "Good dog, FrouFrou, good dog!"

Moments of Distraction

FrouFrou is now our four-legged compass and our GPS in the labyrinth. Why are we blindly following him? Why not? What do we have to lose? Whose path is he following? The Minotaur's? The Minotaur's victims'? My grandfather Virgil's? None of the above?

One good thing about him, something that comforts me, is that he seems to know where he's going. He hasn't once led us to a DEAD END, and we've been walking for about an hour. Now and then we hear the Minotaur's **howls**. But it's impossible to figure out where they are coming from. Is the beast close or not? We fear it will POP UP around each bend or that it will sneak up behind us.

Everyone is on edge, including the dog.

"What do we do if we run into the **MINOTAUR?**" Musky asks.

We freeze.

KABILLIONS of crusty-clawed crawfish in that Bulstrode River! What *will* we do? I look for an answer in my friends' eyes.

"I'll take care of it, Billy Stuart!" Yeti brags. "Bring it on! No, really, bring *it* on!"

The rest of the Zintrepids are silent. As the French would say, they would be stuck to my lips (if I had any).

Don't worry. Being stuck to someone's lips isn't literal! The expression means to listen with attention.

"FrouFrou!" Foxy cries.

The dog has forged ahead while Foxy wasn't paying attention and is barking his way up the passage.

"Quick! He's our only chance to get out of this labyrinth! **Heel**, dirty mutt!"

I don't need to tell you who is talking...

Already he is out of sight. We run ahead, forgetting all about being CAREFUL and putting ourselves at risk of banging into the walls. The gap between us and FrouFrou grows. After making a right turn, we **stop** at a junction. Three new openings present themselves. FrouFrou's barks are getting fainter. I explode.

"Come here, FrouFrou! Please! Don't be so **stubborn!** If I catch you..."

"Instead of getting angry," Foxy reprimands, "we need to figure out which way he went. To the LEFT, straight ahead or to the RIGHT?"

Each moment we hesitate, the poodle gets farther away.

"He must have left his signature scent somewhere," Shifty says.

"You're right! Foxy, out of all of us you have the best nose."

Billy Stuart is correct. The fox's sense of smell is highly developed. A fox can smell the tracks of a hare several hours after it's passed.

"He's your dog, Billy Stuart," she pleads. "You should be able to recognize his odor."

"He's not **MY** dog, and you are wasting precious minutes."

The discussion is postponed until later. Foxy, for the good of the group, puts aside her **ego** and gets down on the ground to sniff.

"Pewww! Stinks of ammonia. That's good. This way," she announces, pointing toward the entrance to our right.

I pick up my pace.

"**Troop, let's hurry!**"

FrouFrou's barking stops. A terrible thought crosses my mind. What if the urine Foxy smelled isn't from the dog, but from the Minotaur? Foxy would be leading us right to the lion's den.

Suddenly I sense something. As if someone is watching us.

A scream explodes:

GRAAAAAOOOOOOOARRRR!

Whatever I sensed sure made a lot of noise! And the screaming was very close. You would swear that it came from the other side of the stone wall.

"Let's stay together," I say to my friends. We slowly move forward.

OOOOOOOOOOOH!

We reach a vast circular room with multiple openings. It is as if all the labyrinth's passages have led us to this very sinister spot.

Get yourself to the heart of the city's maze, my grandfather Virgil wrote in the message in his notebook.

"Here we are in the heart of the mazes!"

A Shadow

Luckily for us, this isn't the Minotaur's stomping grounds, but unluckily for me, there is a poodle that won't quit **jumping up**.

Numerous ***flaming*** torches hang over the entrances, illuminating the biggest room in the labyrinth that we've seen. I keep waiting for the monster to attack us from one of the entrances—or exits, depending on your route.

I ***JUMP*** as I suddenly feel a presence behind me. And again as it disappears just as suddenly...

Shifty, did you see something?

No, Billy Stuart, but I'm keeping my eyes open in all directions.

There, a shadow!
Where there?

Troop, be on guard, we are being watched.

Bring it on! No, really, bring it on!

Are...are they ghosts?

The souls of the Minotaur's victims, haunting the labyrinth.

Prepare to shoot.
!!!

!!!
My odor won't work on ghosts!

They are trying to split us up.

Then we hear a woman's voice:

"Ah, there you are! It's about time."

A silhouette emerges from a door in front of us.

"It's coming! Let's vamoose!"

As soon as he sees the young woman, the poodle runs toward her, barking and jumping for joy.

In the light of the torches, her face is revealed. With her dark **BLACK EYES**, she doesn't need to introduce herself—she must be the sister of Loslobos, the captain of the ship.

"Timoree!" yells Foxy. "You're alive!"

"No," says Musky. "She's dead! It's a ghost! Let's go!"

Timoree does have a corpselike pallor—no doubt because of the lack of sunshine—which is amplified by the large white robe she is wearing.

She comes toward us, looking stunned.

Woof! Woof!

"You...you know me?"

Briefly I explain how.

"My brother hasn't forgotten me," she says, obviously moved.

"How have you survived?" asks Foxy, with FrouFrou back at her side.

Timoree sighs. "It's a long story."

She sees me and suddenly looks horrified.

"**RED**! You're wearing **RED**!" She's panicking.

"Um...yes. So?"

Nervously she looks around the room. "He attacks everything that is **RED**!"

"Like a bull," says Shifty. "He sees **RED**!"

All of a sudden I realize why the victims-to-be were made to wear a piece of **RED** clothing.

The chameleon is wrong. Bulls, along with all other cattle, are color-blind. The color red doesn't annoy the animal. It's the movement of the toreador's cape that irritates the bull. The cape is red for the gruesome purpose of masking the blood left on the cloth from the bull's wounds.

However, in this story, with the Minotaur being half man and half animal, we may presume that he can distinguish red, which is unfortunate for the Zintrepids. As for the expression to see red, it means to have a wild temper. More bad news for our friends.

"**KABILLIONS** of crusty-clawed crawfish in that Bulstrode River!"

My throat feels tight. The red handkerchief around my neck! An **ESSENTIAL** part of the Zintrepids' uniform.

"Troop, we need to take off our scarves! Immediately!"

As I am the one with the most manual dexterity, the members of the pack form a line in front of me for **OPERATION UNTIE RED SCARF**. Timoree lends a helping hand. I untie Foxy's and Yeti's knots while she does Musky's and Shifty's. Shifty, standing next to the young woman, turns as pale as her robe.

We all put our scarves in our backpacks. The torches flicker. Someone with angry **HEAVY BREATHING** has just entered the room.

The Monster Who Sees Red

The Minotaur **BELLOWS**, and the walls shake as foam flies from his mouth.

"Musky, you could spray him!"

"I would love to, but I don't have enough odor left," she says.

"In all this time you haven't recharged?"

"No, I have to be patient for a whole week before I fill back up."

"It's been a millennia since you sprayed the BLACK BEAR! And if this keeps up, we might not be here next week."

The Minotaur looks exactly like I've seen him drawn in books—bull's head, man's body, clothed in a **LOINCLOTH**.

However, he is much bigger than I expected. He is at least three meters tall! We'll only be a mouthful for this monstrous giant. An appetizer before the main meal of Athenians!

"Bring it on! No, really, bring *it* on!" yells Yeti. "Finally, a worthy adversary!"

Musky isn't able to grab him by the collar in time. The weasel charges the Minotaur, jumping onto his leg. His little arms barely wrap around the Minotaur's ankle.

"I have him! I have him!" Yeti yells. "He's at my mercy! Don't worry about him! He's just a big man-cow!"

The Minotaur doesn't even register Yeti's presence. What will the Minotaur do next? His BIG brown eyes fix on…me! Why me?

"Your skirt!" yells Timoree. "Get rid of that skirt!"

"It's not—it's a kilt!"

"Okay, but it's a **RED** kilt!" the young woman points out.

The red color in our friend's kilt—as well as the green—is associated with the Stuart clan (also Stewart). If he were named MacArthur, the predominant color in the tartan would be green (with a pattern of black and yellow lines). Billy MacArthur would not have a problem with the Minotaur.

PROBLEM

NO PROBLEM

How did we remember the scarves but forget such an important detail? Desperately I turn toward…FrouFrou!

"Go on, dog! Attack! Attack! **Grrrrrr…grrrrrr! Skissss! Skissss!** It's only a mail carrier dressed as a Minotaur for Halloween."

"That's stupid, Billy Stuart." Foxy says, getting angry.

"Be careful!" warns Musky.

Just like a bull in a **bullfight**, the Minotaur comes for me, head lowered, horns ready to attack.

"Don't worry, Billy Stuart! I'll hold him back," Yeti says, still clutching the leg of the monster.

The Minotaur draws nearer and nearer, ready to gore me. He comes at me from the right, and I dodge danger by a hair.

"**OLÉ!**" cry the members of my pack from the shelter of one of the passages.

"Toreador! Be careful!" cries Foxy.

Carried forward by his momentum, the beast slips and skids across the floor. This gives me a chance to escape. I try to put as much distance as I can between the Minotaur and me. FrouFrou, thinking it is a game, comes along, bounding happily around me.

"This is not the time, you dirty dog! Go away!"

"Come here, FrouFrou!" Foxy orders in a voice loud enough to be heard over the Minotaur's incessant **MOOING**.

The poodle finally obeys the fox, just as the monster returns to **attack**.

"Take off your kilt!" says Timoree. "It's your only chance!"

"**Nooooooooo!**" A raccoon must keep his dignity until the bitter end. "I'd rather die!"

"If you don't reconsider, that's what's gonna happen, Billy Stuart!" says a worried Musky.

I once dared to ask Billy Stuart if he wears anything under his kilt. He answered, "What a gentleman wears beneath his kilt is nobody's business but his. A well-brought-up raccoon is discreet about this subject. But I will say I have to be careful on super-windy days!"

Running in a straight line is not going to work in these circumstances. I **zig zag** around the big room to deter my abominable adversary. My agility more than my speed is what manages to keep me alive. More than once, I switch

direction at the last second, exasperating the Minotaur, who is furious at missing me.

But how long will I be able to delay the inevitable outcome of this confrontation? At some point, I'll be impaled on his horns.

THE FASTEST ZINTREPID

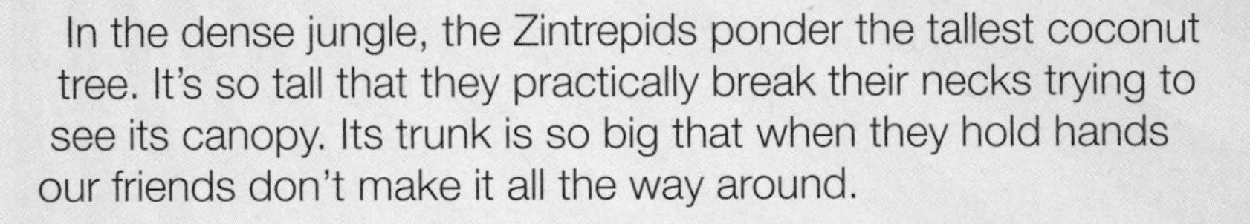

In the dense jungle, the Zintrepids ponder the tallest coconut tree. It's so tall that they practically break their necks trying to see its canopy. Its trunk is so big that when they hold hands our friends don't make it all the way around.

The Zintrepids are starving—they haven't eaten for hours. They wonder who among them, Billy Stuart, Foxy, Musky, Shifty, Yeti or, why not, Froufrou, will be able to climb highest to get a banana.

"Woof! Woof!" barks FrouFrou, Billy Stuart's dog, like he is up for the adventure.

"He's not MY dog!" Billy Stuart, as usual, hurries to point out.

Okay, which of our friends do you think will accomplish this task the fastest? Remember, all of the Zintrepids are able to climb trees.

Your answer will reflect your personality.

Solution on page 159.

With a Little Help from My Friends

I glance at the Zintrepids. Shifty is rummaging in his bag. What is he doing? Oh no!

He has taken his red scarf out and is stretching it out over his body, which instantly takes on its color. The color that attracts the Minotaur's **wrath**.

"I'm creating a diversion! Save yourself, Billy Stuart!"

The red chameleon moves to the middle of the room. The Minotaur spots him, gives up chasing me and starts toward Shifty. Bellowing, the Minotaur charges. Shifty stands as still as a **STATUE**. My friend has no chance. I scream:

"NOOOOOOOOOOO!"

Suddenly Shifty throws his **scarf** as far as he can and lays down. His body takes on the brown color of the marble floor. To the Minotaur, it is as if his target has vanished into thin air. He hits the brakes right in front of my **COURAGEOUS** companion without detecting his presence. The chameleon has simply melted into the decor.

Yeti, who has a ringside seat, waves and gives Shifty a victorious thumbs-up. It is a temporary **victory** that allows us to catch our breath. But I'm not out of danger for long.

The Minotaur lifts his face toward the sky and let out a LOOOOOOOONG cry. He lowers his massive head—and spots me in the corner of the room. He paws powerfully at the floor, then gallops in my direction. I have no choice. Shifty risked his life for me. There goes my **DIGNITY!**

With a sweeping gesture *I* would qualify as courageous, I undo my belt to take off my kilt.

"Throw it!" Foxy implores.

"Okay, Troop! But don't look!" I say to my friends, who are definitely not listening to me.

I **SPIN** my kilt over my head before hurling it toward the center of the room. Then the unthinkable happens. That imbecile of a dog, whose name I won't mention, runs to fetch the kilt. He gets it in his mouth and comes back toward me to return it, with the Minotaur on his heels!

"Let go, FrouFrou!" Foxy commands.

The poodle doesn't hear her—he is too focused on playing a game of fetch with me. I'll have to save myself all over again.

What a ridiculous scene! The **MINOTAUR** is chasing a dog who is trying to catch a half-dressed raccoon. I lean to the **RIGHT** to confuse the monster, then lean to the **LEFT**. But FrouFrou is following me like a shadow and is either going to trip me up or slow me down.

Without stopping, I try to take the kilt out of his jaws.

"Give it to me, you four-legged **POM-POM**! Give it to me!"

"Billy Stuart, stop insulting him!" Foxy cries. "Please, FrouFrou, give it to me!"

I don't dare pull the kilt away for fear of the fabric getting damaged by the poodle's FANGS. I see the monster getting ready to charge again.

I FLICK FrouFrou's nose. He gives a plaintive cry, drops the kilt and runs to find comfort in Foxy's arms.

I resume my run around the room, my kilt in my hands instead of around my waist. This time, I know it'll be the final act.

Meathead!

With that imbecile FrouFrou now safely sheltered with Foxy, the Minotaur has only me to focus on. He is absolutely captivated by the color of my kilt.

I stop skirting the walls and make a direct run right toward the center of the room. My plan could work, but I know I won't get a second chance. It's now or never.

"Shake a leg, Billy Stuart!" Musky cries. "He's practically on top of you!"

Yes, thank you for reminding me. I quickly glance behind me. I wait a little, just a little…

There!

I throw my kilt into the air. Instead of landing on the floor, it gets hooked onto one of the Minotaur's horns. The **monster** stops abruptly. The kilt hangs in front of his eyes. Drawn to it like iron to a magnet, the monstrous beast **dashes** forward, his view partially obstructed.

This way, meathead!
GRRRRR
POK
Olé!
This belongs to me!
You must be pretty bullheaded yourself to have tried that, Billy Stuart!

To be "bullheaded" means to be particularly stubborn. Whether Billy Stuart was being stubborn or just trying to stay alive is up for debate.
I told you guys that I would take care of it.
Does anyone have a camera?
Grmmlgrrrr...
!!!

GRMLLGRRR...
Troop, we can't stay here!
What about the clue, Billy Stuart?
We don't have a second to lose. Let's get out of here lickety split!
And go where? It's impossible to know our way in the labyrinth.
There's our compass!
WOOF!
Our what?
Our ticket out.
Find the exit, dog!
Find the exit, please, my gorgeous FrouFrou.

The poodle sniffs the ground, searching, and then dashes off toward a passage a few meters to the left. He yaps all the while, as if saying, "**Come with me!**" Of course, we follow him.

Before **PLUNGING** myself deeper down the hallway, I look back one last time at the big room. What is the meaning of Grandfather Virgil's clue, *in the heart of the city's maze*?

WARNING! The Minotaur is trying to get back up. He has a huge goose egg on his forehead. With one knee on the ground, he feebly starts to get up. Once on his legs, he staggers around. When he sees that we're gone, he **SHRIEKS** in fury. He lurches a few steps in my direction. And then, as if pulled by an invisible cord, he trips all over again. It's clear that he has not regained all his senses.

"Go on, troop! We must not dillydally!"

I turn around quickly—and discover that I'm *alone*! They haven't waited for me.

The Exploit

KABILLIONS of crusty-clawed crawfish in that Bulstrode River! Here I am, lost in the labyrinth **again**!

It's **IRONIC**. After my fighting and flooring the Minotaur, after my saving the lives of my companions, they've abandoned me like an **OLD SET OF BAGPIPES**. They've escaped without me, guided by a dog whom *I* have looked after day and night and on whom *I* have wasted the best days of my summer holiday.

BUNCH OF INGRATES!

How will I find the exit now? The passages all look exactly the same. If I choose the wrong direction, I might end up wandering around inside here for the rest of my days, and I

have no doubt that the monster will keep looking for me. But if I stay put, the end result…will likely be the same.

The anxiety I feel at this outcome is making it hard to think. That and the Minotaur's incessant mooing…

Wait! I have an idea. I should be able to smell FrouFrou's trail. There must still be a scent.

I squat and try to detect the YOU-KNOW-WHAT at the base of the walls. Preoccupied by my olfactory research, I don't hear the beast behind me.

I jump when I spot him…leaping with joy on his hind legs.

"Here you are!" Foxy rejoices. "I thought you'd gotten lost, my **adorable** little treasure."

If I were Shifty hearing this, my skin would have turned the color of my kilt. But Foxy's words warm my heart, her calling me her **adorable** treasure.

Me too! I'm happy to see you!!!
Ah! Billy Stuart! Because of you, we wasted time and almost lost FrouFrou!
I'm happy to see you too, Foxy.
You can thank Musky. She's the one who noticed you were gone.
And your dog found you. He deserves some thanks.
He's not my d—
That's enough! Let's go!
Get us out of here, my beautiful FrouFrou, please.
Troop, let's stay together this time around.

Our race (we certainly are not walking) through the DARK corridors seems like it is never going to end. The Minotaur's grunts are getting louder, a sure sign that he's getting closer. And we have started to slow down because the poodle, who was in such a hurry before, has lost his trail and has to find it again. Which is very annoying.

I have the SINKING feeling that we've been going in circles for the last few minutes.

What a **mistake!**

The dog is right! Daylight at the end of a passageway shows us our way out. We emerge from the labyrinth, dazzled by the sun beating down on the entrance.

“It’s the first time someone has come out **ALIVE!**”

The rumor of our feat spreads like a puff of smoke throughout the city.

Like a *puff of smoke* means "very quickly."

People are gathering around the labyrinth, hoping to witness this **extraordinary** event. The king, alerted to our feat, promptly arrives with his armed guards and sends for the Athenian prisoners.

In front of this cheering crowd, I congratulate myself on having remembered to put my kilt back on! Appearing half dressed in public would have been terribly humiliating.

A New Threat

Once the surprise has worn off, Ronos, guardian of the labyrinth, is overjoyed! King Minos will have to give him the hand of his daughter and his fortune, because someone has conquered the ultimate test of the labyrinth. At last his big day has arrived!

The king, followed by his guard, comes over to us, suspiciously happy. Ronos says hello to a young woman with long black hair, who is behind them. She is no doubt his bride to be.

Behind them the Athenians, clothed in red, are assembled. They will be fed to the Minotaur over the next few days. Among them I spot Zeppelinos, obviously happy to see us alive.

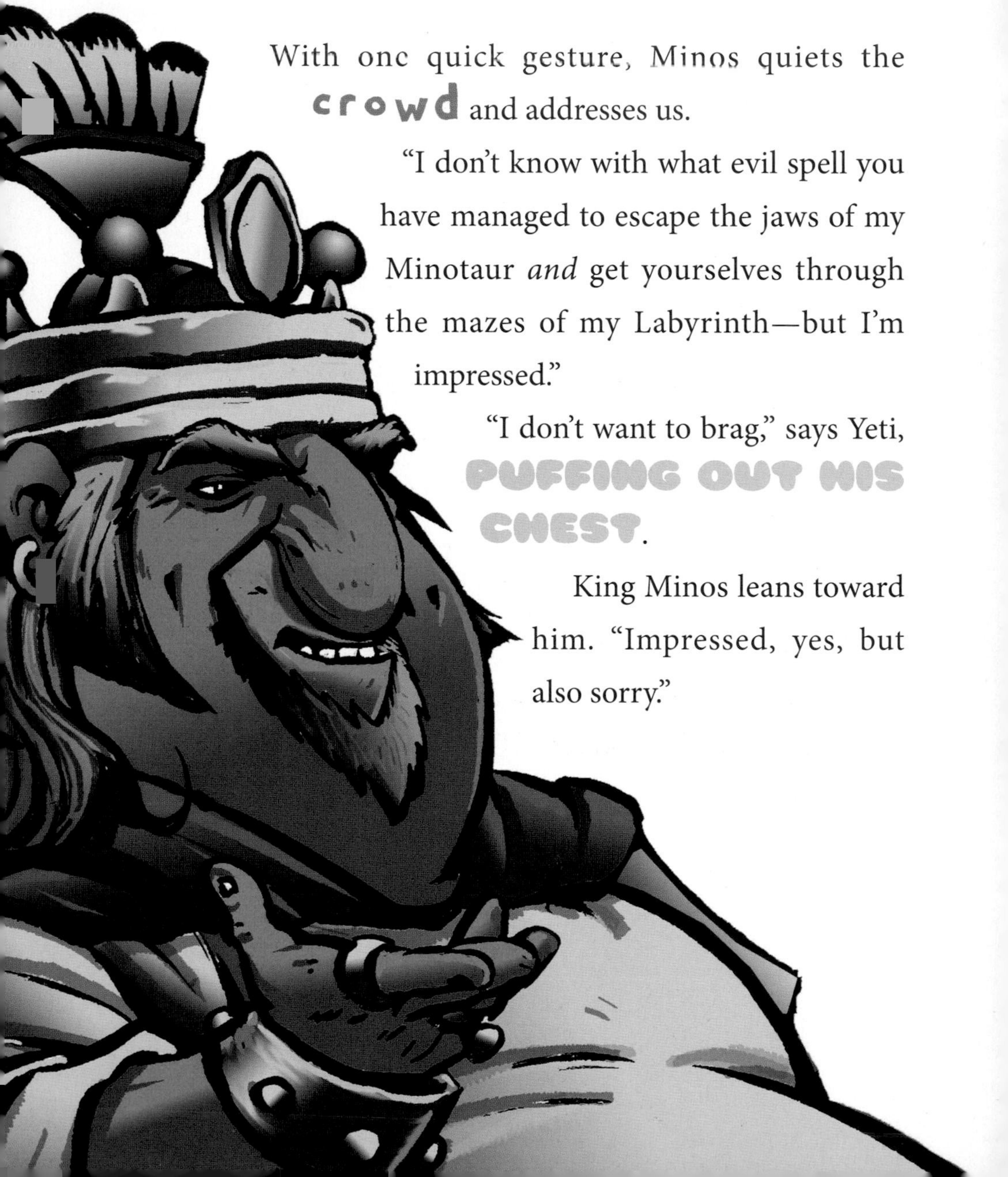

With one quick gesture, Minos quiets the **crowd** and addresses us.

"I don't know with what evil spell you have managed to escape the jaws of my Minotaur *and* get yourselves through the mazes of my Labyrinth—but I'm impressed."

"I don't want to brag," says Yeti, **PUFFING OUT HIS CHEST**.

King Minos leans toward him. "Impressed, yes, but also sorry."

"Sorry? Why?"

He SNAPS his fingers, and the soldiers approach, pushing the Athenians ahead of them.

"Sorry because now I have to do what the Minotaur was not able to. It's a question of safeguarding our reputation in the modern world. The gods will be angry if they don't receive their gift. And since the labyrinth is our principal tourist attraction, you must understand that letting you live would force me to change my ingenious motto *When you go in, you never go out!*"

With the tips of their spears, the guards push us back against the wall of the labyrinth.

"Him too!" the king orders, pointing at Ronos.

Minos's daughter objects. "Father! You can't do that!" she says, in tears. "You promised us!"

I'm standing at the entrance to the labyrinth. I tell the Athenians to take off their red robes and throw them to the ground. Without questioning me, they do. I plead with Zeppelinos to give me his. The king doesn't suspect anything and seems to think I am being thrifty.

King Minos starts to stammer as the Minotaur barrels out of the labyrinth. The crowd is **SHOCKED**. The soldiers lower their spears and back away from the entrance.

The Minotaur is **blinded** by the sun and tries to shield his eyes.

"No one move," I say.

I throw Zeppelinos's red robe into the air, which, helped along by a stiff breeze, lands...on the king's head.

The Minotaur, with an awful bellow, hurls himself toward Minos, causing **PANIC** in the crowd. The people flee—all except the king, who can't see a thing.

He rips the robe from his head. Frustrated and red with fury, he yells, "Who dares attack a king?"

Red with fury, yellow belly, seeing life through rose-colored glasses, having the blues...several expressions are associated with color. The poor king will soon be white—with fright!

The king looks up and sees the Minotaur just a few short centimeters from his face. With one robust swipe the Minotaur seizes his royal prey, who is now **hysterical**, and flings him onto his shoulders. Then he retreats to the solitude of his labyrinth.

The Athenians and Zintrepids take advantage of the chaos to escape to the PORT OF KNOSSOS.

Safe and Sound

Are we fugitives? Traveling with the Athenians, should we use less-traveled paths? Nope! In Knossos, the rumor is that people want to be free of the Minotaur. Those who are either SCARED or wise stay home. Those who consider themselves BRAVE head toward the labyrinth, swords in hand. They want to liberate the city from the monster and make history. And those people who are CURIOUS can't resist running toward the spectacle just to see what will happen.

At this moment we have nothing to worry about—the main roads are completely free of anyone!

"We are free!" Timoree cheers.

Incredulously I ask, "Free?"

My Zintrepids troop knows exactly why I seem incredulous. Can we really be *free* when we've landed in a strange land after **time traveling**, going thousands of years back in time?

At this stage of our adventure, the only difference between the labyrinth and our current path is that there are no monsters on our tail. Is it our DESTINY to be on this Greek island forever? Should we leave by boat? Where should we go? Is it even possible to return home to the twenty-first century without the clue we were meant to find in *the heart of the city's maze*?

The only thing we have brought back from our stay in the labyrinth is Timoree. And she isn't a *thing*, much less a clue.

"With a little luck, your brother's ship will still be docked," I tell her.

"Timoree, how did you survive in the labyrinth?" asks Musky.

"Ah, that's a long story. I managed to..."

The young woman abruptly stops her story when we reach the top of a hill, where we have a magnificent view

of the port of Knossos. She recognizes the boat of her brother, Captain Loslobos.

"Yes, he *is* there! Let's hurry!"

She races down the slope so fast she's in danger of hurting herself.

Once on the wharf, she frantically searches for her brother aboard the ship. He has his back to us, facing the sea. Timoree cries his name and waves frantically.

"Loslobos! Loslobos!"

The captain swings around. His whole being explodes with joy.

"Timoree! Timoree!"

The brother and sister reunite on the gangplank and throw their arms around each other.

Tears flow abundantly. Reunions are so moving!

We climb aboard the ship, and the captain welcomes us as heroes.

"Ah! My friends! Thank you for saving my sister. I will be forever in your debt. This boat is your boat."

"COOL! I'll drive!" Yeti says enthusiastically.

"Cast off!" orders the captain. "We're going home!"

The Clue

We don't need to use the **oars** for the return trip to Athens. The wind vigorously blows the sails, which are white now. As a tribute to his sister, Loslobos has pulled down the **black sails** and replaced them with these, which are more appropriate for the celebration.

Ugobos, the slave guard, is in a bad mood. It makes him very unhappy that we have become friends with the captain. He wants to avoid our company altogether.

At dinner we are seated at the captain's **TABLE**. I get comfortably tucked in to the left of Timoree. Our adventures have given me an appetite. Am I ever hungry!

We still don't know how the young woman survived the labyrinth. But that's the least of my worries. I don't care if she ate **rats** or **ROACHES** or if she spent weeks drinking rainwater.

Roaches are cockroaches. If you cut off one's head, it stays alive for a week. Creepy, right?

"Timoree, when we first ran into you in the big room, why did you say 'it's about time'?"

EMBARRASSED, she hides her face in her hands.

"You're right, Billy Stuart. That was not a very polite way to greet my rescuers."

"You were waiting for us to arrive? How is that possible?"

Silence falls around the table. My companions lean in to listen to our conversation—all except for Yeti, who is too busy recounting his exploits to the captain.

"One of your...**UM**"—she tries to think of the correct word—"companions accompanied my group to the labyrinth. He looked like you, Billy Stuart, but he was quite a bit older."

"**KABILLIONS** of crusty-clawed crawfish in that Bulstrode River!"

My grandfather, Virgil?
He didn't tell me his name, but I assure you, he showed an unusual amount of courage and generosity.
As soon as he entered the labyrinth, he volunteered to take the place of a young sick boy and certainly saved his life.
That's my grandfather, a hero in the noblest sense of the word!

Timoree takes a **mouthful of wine**, gargles, fills her cheeks and swallows. Then she starts her story again.

"Your grandfather, Billy Stuart, understood that the **MINOTAUR** was attracted to the color red. But I was the only one who listened. Once I was inside the labyrinth, I wore my white robe and was the only survivor."

And my grandfather?
He disappeared the day after he promised that someone would come to take me out of that trap.
I don't know what happened to him.
He knew what he was doing.
A toast to the health of Billy Stuart's grandfather.
CLINK
Your grandfather gave me this pebble.
!?!?
I was told to give it to the person who saved me. He assured me that whoever that was would know what to do.
It looks like a piece of coal.
What is it?
!?!

I rummage in my backpack and take out the **leather notebook**. I open it and leaf through. There is the map, roughly sketched, and the message from my grandfather. I stop at the page after that, which is blank, and darken it by rubbing it with the **coal**.

"What is this?" the captain asks as my grandfather's handwriting reveals itself.

I read out loud:

"If you have this message in hand, it's because you're following my footsteps. **BRAVO**, Billy Stuart! The Minotaur was a good introduction to your voyage, don't you think? For what's next, you need to go beyond the sea, and confront **A THOUSAND DANGERS**, before you can find the way home. It will be a big change from mowing the **LAWN** or walking the dog, won't it?"

I shoot a grumpy look at the poodle, who is sitting beside me, wagging his tail.

"Who knows," teases Shifty. "One day someone will write your story and call it *The Adventures of Billy Stuart and FrouFrou*!"

The Zintrepids burst out laughing, and the dog resumes dancing in place.

In *The Adventures of Tintin*, the creator, Hergé, titled one of his stories "The adventures of Tintin and Snowy." The idea of putting FrouFrou's name with Billy Stuart's for the cover of the books tempted me. I discussed it with him. He outright refused. Are you surprised?

With this poodle dancing around my feet, I can't shake the feeling that I'm going to be doing a lot of homework while on this adventure.

"What does your grandfather mean?" asks Timoree. "What voyage is he speaking of? And what does 'mow the lawn' mean? Is it one of your expressions?"

I ***sigh*** and hang my head. "That too is a long story."

"We're all ears," says Loslobos.

He and his sister will never believe this. **Oh well!**

Pointing to my troops, I say:

"You may have noticed that this is not our home. Truthfully, we come from the future—"

I'm cut short by a sailor entering the cabin.

Captain! A storm is rising on the horizon! We need to change our course to avoid it.

SEARCH AND FIND

Can you find these elements in the book?

Solution on page 159.

SOLUTIONS

TOPSY-TURVY (P. 22)

Here is one possible solution
fear–dear–deal–meal

ANAGRAMS (P. 34)

minos–simon / team–tame / swaps–wasps / looped–poodle / master–stream

THE ENIGMA (P. 72)

There are several possible solutions. Here is one:

Musky and Shifty are the first ones to get on board the boat. They cross the river.

Shifty debarks, and Musky comes back.

Musky debarks, and Foxy and Yeti cross.

Foxy and Yeti debark.

Shifty crosses and gets Musky.

Musky and Shifty cross.

Shifty debarks, and Musky goes back across for Billy Stuart.

Musky debarks, and Billy Stuart crosses.

Shifty comes back and gets Musky.

The two cross, and the game is finished.

THE FASTEST ZINTREPID (P. 112)

If you have chosen Billy Stuart, you are the kind who likes to lead a group. People naturally follow you. But, sadly, this is not the correct solution.

If you answered Foxy, you are a trickster. You know how to arrive at your destination. People call you a fox. Sadly, you are not correct.

If you believe it's Musky, you are tenacious. You don't let go until you have reached your goal, no matter the obstacles. But you're wrong this time.

If you see Shifty being the first on high, you are like him: patient and clever. You don't hesitate to take the necessary time to do things well. Clever or not, you have missed your target.

If you opt for Yeti, it's because you are a veritable bundle of energy. No challenge will stop you. Not even those that interest us. Still, we can't count on the weasel to finish this task.

Lastly, if you chose FrouFrou—and you are allowed to, after all—you are everybody's friend. Except Billy Stuart's, just to warn you.

So? If you concluded that none of the Zintrepids would succeed in this mission, you are brilliant! Bravo! You are right! You know that at the top of a coconut tree, there are no bananas growing!

SEARCH AND FIND (PP. 156–157)

SCORPION, PAGE 44
TREE, PAGE 30
SCARF, PAGE 115
MAN, PAGE 57
COOKING POT, PAGE 148
TORCH, PAGE 68
SEAGULL, PAGE 52
FISH, PAGE 152
WHEEL, PAGE 61
LANTERN, PAGE 152

A prolific author, Alain M. Bergeron has written over 250 children's books. He devotes himself exclusively to writing and leading school workshops. His inexhaustible imagination has made him a fixture in children's literature, and he has received many awards and accolades. Alain lives in Victoriaville, Quebec.

Multitalented, self-taught illustrator and cartoonist Samuel Parent, better known by the pen name Sampar, possesses a lively imagination that draws viewers into worlds that are moving, wacky and sometimes even mythical. He lives in Victoriaville, Quebec.